JUST RIGHT

Written by

ALAN OSMOND

Illustrated by

THOMAS AARESTAD

A TWICE UPON A TIME TALE

Goldilocks and The Three Bears

Published by Ideals Children's Books
An imprint of Hambleton-Hill Publishing, Inc.
Nashville, Tennessee 37218

Library of Congress Cataloging-in-Publication Data
Osmond, Alan
Just Right/ by Alan Osmond; illustrated by Thomas Aarrestad. —1st ed.
p.   cm. (Twice upon a time)
Summary: Junior Bear is missing, and Goldie, the police officer sent to investigate his disappearance, looks oddly familiar to Junior's family.
ISBN 1-57102-132-9 (hardcover)
[1. Characters in literature—Fiction. 2. Missing children—Fiction. 3. Bears—Fiction.] I. Aarrestad, Thomas, ill. II. Title. III. Series: Osmond, Alan. Twice upon a time.
PZ.08345Ju 1998
[E]—dc21   98-16586
CIP
AC

First Edition

Written by Alan Osmond
Illustrated by Thomas Aarrestad

Cover and book design LaughlinStudio

ALAN OSMOND

Suzanne and I dedicate this book to our eight sons:

Michael, Nathan, Douglas, David, Scott, Jon, Alex,

and Tyler. . .a.k.a. The Osmonds—Second Generation.

When telling our boys bedtime stories, the concept

came that the classics can also live on for

a second generation and could be told not only once,

but "Twice Upon A Time."

THOMAS AARRESTAD

To Olivia.

Twice upon a time, on the outskirts of a small city, there lived a family of bears. Tiny, his wife Suzy, and their son, Junior, shared a house in the woods with Tiny's parents, Grandma and Grandpa Bear.

5

One day, Tiny and Suzy couldn't find their son. They looked high and low and everywhere in between. Tiny checked with Grandma and Grandpa Bear.

"Have you seen Junior?" asked Tiny.

"No, we haven't," they said.

Suzy went to their neighbors and friends and asked, "Has anyone seen our Junior?"

But no one had seen Junior all day!

"Where, oh where could he be?" cried Suzy.

"We've looked everywhere!" said Grandma Bear.

"We'd better call 911," said Grandpa Bear.

Tiny dialed the telephone and said, "Hello, this is Tiny calling. Our son Junior is missing and nobody knows where he is. Please help us find him!"

The emergency operator said, "We will send a police officer to your house immediately!"

Soon the bear family saw a uniformed policeman on a mountain bike coming up the forest path to their house. The policeman knocked on the door and Grandpa Bear grumpily invited him in.

When he took off his helmet, they discovered it wasn't a man after all! It was a young woman with beautiful, straight, golden hair.

"Thank you for coming so quickly," said Tiny. He scratched his chin thoughtfully. "You look very familiar. Have we met you before?"

"I don't think so," said the policewoman. "My name is Goldie and I'm new to the police force." She took a notebook out of her back pocket. "Now, please tell me about your missing son."

Goldie gathered as much information as she could about Junior and said, "I will get back to you as soon as I learn anything." She looked around the house, shook her head, and then hurried out the front door.

"I know I've seen her before, but I can't quite remember where," said Grandpa Bear.

"Yes," Grandma Bear agreed. "It should be so easy to remember someone with all that golden hair!"

9

Goldie decided to do a little investigating around the Bears' house. She noticed a set of paw prints leading out of the forest and she was going to follow them when it suddenly began to rain. She hurried back to the police station.

When she got there, the captain told her that there was trouble at the local hotel. Goldie told her boss about the little footprints in the forest and asked if she could be the one assigned to check out the hotel.

"I have a feeling that I might find some clues that will lead us to Junior," she said.

The captain told her to be careful and walked her to the door. She was in such a hurry to get to the hotel that she forgot her umbrella and ran straight through the pouring rain.

The hotel manager met her at the front desk. "Somebody broke into the kitchen, the rear lobby, and the penthouse suite," he said. "Whoever it was did some damage and we think he's still in the hotel!"

Goldie said, "Don't worry; I'll find him," and headed for the kitchen.

"Somebody's been eating our food!" said the cook.

He showed her where someone had tipped over a pot of hot chili peppers and taken a bite out of one.

"It's no wonder they only took one bite," said Goldie. "These thing are really hot!"

Next Goldie noticed some potato soup on the floor.

"Hmmm ," she said. "Whoever tasted this doesn't like their soup cold."

Then she noticed a pile of pizza crusts on the floor in the corner of the room.

She said, "But somebody sure loves pizza. They ate the whole thing!"

The hotel manager took Goldie to the rear lobby. "Somebody's been sitting in our chairs!" said the bellboy, pointing at a big oak bench.

Goldie noticed scratch marks and fuzzy hairs on the bench. "Somebody doesn't like to sit on such a hard bench," she said.

The bellboy pointed out a large, fluffy sofa.

"Look how the cushion has been ripped open," said Goldie. "Somebody sure doesn't like fluffy things. They've thrown sofa stuffing all over the place!"

And then, near the elevator, she saw a little love seat. It had been jumped in by dirty little feet and turned upside down.

"Somebody small really liked this chair. They smeared pizza sauce all over it!"

Goldie wrote down all the things she'd discovered in her notebook. She was beginning to see a pattern in the way the intruder was behaving.

oldie, the manager, the bellboy, and the cook rode the elevator up to the penthouse suite. The maid was waiting for them by the door. "Somebody's been sleeping in our beds!" she said.

"I knew it!" said Goldie.

She walked into the room and up to the king-sized bed. "Just as I thought! Somebody small tried to climb up here. It was too high, and they ended up pulling the quilt off. They must be getting tired."

G oldie looked around the room carefully and then said, "Let me guess . . ."
She went into the powder room and looked down into the sunken bath tub. The quilt was lying at the bottom.

"I was right!" she said. She looked at the manager, the maid, the bellboy, and the cook. "Somebody doesn't like the feeling of being stuck in a place that's down too low."

hey all walked back into the middle of the bedroom. Goldie reviewed the notes she'd made and said:

"Hmmm. Too hot...too cold...just right.

"Hmmm. Too hard...too fluffy...just right.

"Hmmm. Too high...too low..."

She slowly opened the closet door and shouted, "Too bad! I gotcha!"

There, cuddled up on the cozy closet carpet, was Junior! Goldie started to laugh.

ust as Junior opened his eyes a bright flash of lightning lit up the penthouse suite. A loud crash of thunder followed, and Junior clapped his hands over his ears, stood up, and let out a young bear's roar.

Before Goldie could react, he was out the door, down the stairs, and running away from the hotel as fast as his little legs could carry him.

Tiny, Suzy, and Grandma and Grandpa Bear were very happy to see the soaking wet, scared cub when he finally made it home. He was just finishing the story of his adventures when there was a knock at the front door.

"Don't answer it!" Junior shouted.

Tiny slowly opened the door. There stood Goldie, drenched and out of breath. Her once straight hair was now a mass of golden curls. Tiny stared at her for a moment and then invited her in.

Tiny turned his attention back to Junior.

"It is wrong to not let your parents know where you are going," he said.

"It is also wrong to go into other people's places uninvited," said Suzy.

"And it is wrong to take their food," added Grandma Bear.

"It is wrong to use their things, too," said Grandpa Bear.

They all turned to Goldie and said,
"Isn't that right…Goldilocks?"
Goldie's face turned almost as bright red as Junior's.

"I'm sorry for what I did," said Junior.

"Me too," said Goldie, and they all laughed about
what had happened once upon a time.

THE END